Peter Wee
&
The First Aid Kit

by
Karen Ruth Yaxley

Brigand
London

Brigand Press,
All contact: info@brigand.london

British Library Cataloguing-in-Publication Data
A catalogue record for this book is available from the British Library

Printed and Bound in Great Britain by
Datum Creative Media Limited
www.datum.agency

ISBN: 978-1-912978-31-1

ACKNOWLEDGEMENTS

A huge thank you to my sister Paula, for firstly listening on Skype during lockdown to the next chapter, as well as proof reading and sorting out my grammar, as I am definitely somewhat dyslexic.

Thank you too to my artistic mother, who at the tender age of 87, completed all the amazing illustrations for this book and passed on some very useful, practical and creative skills to me over the years.

A special thanks to my sister Debbie, for sitting, listening and laughing at the correct times to me reading aloud.

To my two wonderful nieces, Emily & Imogen, for legging it every afternoon to walk the dog during lockdown, while I skyped their mother to read a far too childish book for them to listen to.

And finally, to my parents for their patience of bringing up a mischievous and often hilarious and grumpy daughter.

ABOUT THE AUTHOR

Karen Ruth Yaxley lives in Lightwater, Surrey, with her best friend Frankie, a Bearded Collie.

When she was thrown into lockdown during the coronavirus pandemic, she finally had quality time to write her first book, which had been trying to escape her thoughts for the last forty-five years.

Her love of animals large and small, and her vivid imagination from an early age, inspired her to write a magical children's book.

There are still many more chapters waiting to escape. So, hopefully this is only the start of Peter Wee's adventures.

This book is dedicated to my brother-in-law Simon, who sadly has passed from this world, far too young. If Simon had still been around to listen to his mad sister-in-law reading this book aloud, he would have taken great pleasure in teasing her about her continual lack of living in the real world!

A VISIT TO THE PET SHOP

'Ouch,' said Mark, as he promptly put the white guinea pig back down in the straw.

'Mum, I don't want that one, it tried to nibble me.'

Mark and his mum were at his favourite pet shop. He had finally persuaded his parents to let him have a guinea pig, although it was only going to be his seventh birthday. His brother Tom had only been allowed to get his when he was eight, but Mark's mum had given in as he kept complaining, saying he was always hard done by being the youngest child. She just wanted some peace and quiet. The young shop assistant now passed him a smooth-haired brown and white guinea pig.

'This one is definitely a male,' she said.

Mark held him up high, looking under his tummy, although he didn't really know what he was looking for. He had to have a male as Gerald, Tom's guinea pig, was a boy and they would be sharing a hutch. The guinea pig started squeaking *weet, weet, weet*.

'I like this one, mum, I think he likes me. I will call him Peter.'

Mark was so excited. His dad was at home finishing off the posh new hutch that Gerald and Peter would live in, while Benjamin, Debbie's rabbit, would be moved into the old hutch, once inhabited by Gerald. This was much to Debbie, his

elder sister's disgust. She had agreed only on the terms that because she now had more homework, her two brothers were in charge of all regular hutch cleaning duties.

Peter was placed in a cardboard box with some hay and as soon as he was safely stowed away, the young shop assistant gave strict instructions on water and feed. She handed Mark a flyer on "how to care for your guinea pig." Peter also had special bedding, a new water bottle and guinea pig supreme nuggets, bought by his mum as part of his present. It was only ten minutes journey back home in the car, which Peter seemed to enjoy, balanced on Mark's lap. *Weet, weet,* went Peter.

As soon as they were in the drive, Mark jumped out of the car with his precious cargo and ran into the back garden.

'Look, dad,' he cried, 'he's brown and white and called Peter.'

Mark's dad was just putting the finishing touches to the hutch – a pretend chimney no less.

'Keep him in the box for five more minutes Mark and the hutch will be ready.'

Mark stared at the hutch in awe. It had two separate doors, one with a large latch that opened onto the main compartment that was wire meshed. The other door was solid wood. Behind this door there were two floors, an upstairs where Peter and Gerald could sleep and a cosy snug below for chill out time, with a small textured ramp for them to climb between the two. Mark had learnt in the pet shop that guinea pigs only sleep for about four hours a day but needed somewhere they could hide and feel safe.

'Dad, it's amazing. Thank you so much.'

'You're welcome, son, but don't go getting upset tomorrow when you don't have many presents to open. Now go and get some fresh hay from the shed.'

With that, dad lifted the hutch onto a metal frame. He had made it to keep the hutch three feet off the ground, making it easier for the boys to clean. He stood back to admire his work.

'Not bad, if I say so myself.'

Mark scattered the hay thinly in the main hutch and put some of the paper bedding in the two smaller compartments, clipped on the filled water bottle and put some of the nuggets and a few slices of cucumber in the hutch. He carefully lifted Peter out of the box.

'Hello Peter, this is your new home,' he said, stroking him fondly, 'hope you like it.'

He then went to collect Gerald, who was in the wire run that dad had also made, so they could exercise and munch on the grass. However, dad made them move it round the lawn often, as he said the pets ruined the grass. Gerald ran round fast when he saw Mark approaching. He was much bigger than Peter, so Mark managed to catch him quite easily.

'Come and meet your new friend,' Mark said. His dad stood next to him as he popped Gerald in the hutch. 'Peter, meet Gerald.'

Peter ran for cover into the bedding, but within a couple of moments both guinea pigs were whistling at each other. Dad said that was a good sign and we should leave them for a while, while we went and had tea.

Mark promised Peter he would be back soon.

Mark was so excited, not only was he going to be seven tomorrow, it was also the start of the Easter holidays. Two weeks to play with Peter, yippee! His brother Tom had just arrived home

from football practice and his sister Debbie pulled
up a chair for tea. He could not wait to tell them
all about his amazing early birthday present.

 After tea, and after having to dry up, Mark
ran back down to the end of the garden with Tom.
They carefully opened the latch and there were

Peter and Gerald curled up together in the chill out area.

'My flyer said guinea pigs don't like to sleep close together,' Mark said.

'Don't knock it, they look right at home,' Tom said. 'Come on, leave them, they are tired and so are you. You have a special day tomorrow and can play with Peter then.'

They draped an old curtain that their mum had given them over the hutch. There were often foxes in the garden and she said this would put them off the scent. Mark gave out a little yawn, nodded and raced Tom back to the house.

'Yes, I have two weeks of fun,' he thought.

SEVEN TODAY

Mark woke early. He had fidgeted all night but knew not to get too excited as he had received most of his presents yesterday. He checked his watch. It was finally 7.00am, so he could get up now without getting told off. He showered and dressed quickly. As he ran downstairs, he saw a small pile of presents on the table but decided to check on Peter first. He took a tomato and some sliced pepper from the fridge and ran down the garden. As he lifted the curtain off the hutch, Peter and Gerald were looking straight up at him.

'HAPPY BIRTHDAY,' Peter said, 'we thought you were never going to get here.'

Mark stood there with his mouth wide open, dropping the tomato and pepper slices onto the ground.

'GUINEA PIGS don't talk!' he said.

'MAGIC ONES DO!' said Peter.

Mark could not contain his excitement and was jumping up and down on the spot. What an amazing birthday this was turning out to be.

'Peter, did you really speak?'

'Yes Mark, but only you can hear me, the rest of your family will just hear our normal weeting and purring.'

'Oh my,' said Mark, still confused by what he had just observed.

'Thanks for the food, now go and open your presents, we will see you later,' Peter said. 'Happy Birthday!'

Mark walked slowly back into the house, he wouldn't tell anyone, especially Tom as he wouldn't believe him anyway and just get called a silly little brother. It was his secret. His family sat around the breakfast table. In the middle of the table was a sort of white guinea pig shaped birthday cake, with seven candles down its back.

'Sorry, I gave it my best shot, I thought you'd choose a white one as it was easier for me to ice,' his mum said smiling.

'Happy seventh birthday Son,' his parents said.

Mark hugged his mum and dad and sat down at the table. He then unwrapped his presents.

Mum and dad had given him a large bag of various extra supplies for Peter and a book on the Vikings as it was his school project. Tom and Debbie had bought him some of his favourite Lego people and his Auntie Paula and Uncle Andrew a new Nintendo game.

'WOW,' he said, 'I'm so lucky.'

'Don't forget to phone your Auntie and Uncle later,' his mum said.

'No mum, I won't,' said Mark.

Mark tucked into orange juice, a warmed croissant with chocolate spread (one of his favourite things) and a slice of buttered toast.

'As it is my birthday, can I get away without drying up today please? I would like to play with Peter.' Mum nodded.

'Put Gerald in the run for me please,' said Tom, 'I'm going to see my friends at the park.'

Mark ran back down the garden to the hutch. Peter and Gerald were waiting for him.

'Hi, it's me' he said, thinking he must have been dreaming earlier and it would stay quiet.

'Hi,' Peter said back.

'Peter, I have to ask you, why can you speak?' Mark said, 'It's not normal for animals!'

'No,' said Peter, 'I will explain. When I was born, my parents asked me what I would have liked to have been if I wasn't a guinea pig. I said a doctor, as I love helping all my fellow creatures. Mum said she could pass on a special gift to me that she had, to talk to humans. This would help me to help others, as I couldn't do this without the help of kind people. So here I am talking to you.'

'I have another shock for you, Mark. Do you need to sit down?' Peter said.

'No,' said Mark, 'I am SEVEN NOW!'

'Okay, when I arrived and met Gerald, I realised he was a girl. Your brother Tom wouldn't have known, and the shop assistant was young and wanted to keep Tom happy. So, Gerald would be grateful if you call her Geraldine now please.'

'Of course,' said Mark, scratching his head and laughing.

'We would love to stretch our legs a bit in the run please. It's not big enough in the hutch to do my circuits!' Peter said.

Mark got the giggles and couldn't stop laughing.

'Sorry,' Peter said, 'just one more thing. Can you ask your mum to sew us a hammock please, they are all the rage now and are so comfy. Tell her you saw some in the pet shop.'

'Okay,' said Mark.

Mark carefully lifted Peter first, then Geraldine into the run, stroking them as he put them down.

'I really have a very special friend now,' he said, smiling. Mark sat on the corner of the run, watching Geraldine (he would have to get used to her new name) and Peter chasing each other, or doing circuits, as he now knew it was called. After a while Mark went into the kitchen and got some fresh water to put in their bottle and some lettuce leaves. When he asked his mum if she would make a hammock for the hutch, she gave him a very strange look, but said she would if he could show her a picture later. As Mark put the food and water in the run, Peter reminded him to clean out the hutch.

'Okay I'm on it,' said Mark.

Mark tidied the hutch.

'Pooh,' he said, while clearing away the old food and guinea pig mess. He fluffed up the bedding and sat back down on the run.

'Thanks,' Peter said. 'It must be time for our first adventure! Can you pop Benjamin in the run to keep Geraldine company while we are away?'

'Yes,' Mark said, 'but where are we going?'

'You'll see,' said Peter.

THE HAY BALES

'Thanks, Mark,' said Peter. 'Now, put me in your jacket pocket and I'll stay quiet as we go through the house. Let your mum know that you are just going over the road to the field to play in the hay bales, she'll be happy then. She knows farmer James is happy for you to play there.'

'See if you can pick up a sandwich on the way through and don't forget something I like, I'm partial to a red apple if you see one. We'll have to be back by two anyway, ready for your birthday party,' Peter said.

Mum was in the kitchen finishing off some party sandwiches for later. She let Mark take a couple of them and an apple. 'I will be having lots of party food later,' he thought. She smiled and made him promise to be back by 1.45, so he could spruce up for his party.

'Thanks, mum,' he said, as he skipped out the door, thinking, 'spruce up into what?'

The sun was warm on his back, but he had to wear his jacket to carry Peter. He crossed the road looking carefully both ways, although very rarely did he see a car. It was normally just farmer James in his tractor, with his friend Josh hanging on the side. That was the joy of living in the country. Josh was farmer James' son and his best friend. He would see him later at the party. Mark carefully made his way around the edge of the wheat field. It wouldn't be long until harvest, he thought, as the wheat was nearly up to his shoulders.

'Hello, getting a bit warm in here, so could you hold me the rest of the way please,' said Peter.

'Sorry,' said Mark giggling and lifted Peter out of his pocket.

'Phew, fresh air,' Peter said. 'I don't know what you've had in your pocket, but it stinks.'

'Sorry,' Mark said, giggling again.

He had been given a handful of Harry Potter jellybeans by Carl at school the other day but had spat most of them out on the way home, especially the ear wax ones. It made him feel sick just thinking about it. They arrived at a pile of old hay bales and Mark sat down on the driest one he could find.

'You can put me down,' Peter said, 'I'm not going anywhere.' They started chatting like old friends.

'Peter how old are you?' Mark said.

'Just 6 months old in human terms,' Peter said.

'Oh,' said Mark, 'but you're not with your parents and brothers and sisters?'

'No,' said Peter, 'guinea pigs only live until they are aged six or seven, so I am a grown-up already.'

Mark scratched his head. He was quite confused by this information.

'You'll be a teenager by the time I'm seven, so won't have time for me anyway, not by then,' Peter said.

Mark looked concerned.

'Enough of this, we have serious business to deal with. Now pass me my apple please,' asked Peter.

Peter started scrunching on his apple, while Mark tucked into his sandwiches. Just as they were finishing, Peter called out, *Weet, weet.*

'Mark, did you hear that? Something is injured over there.'

Mark jumped to his feet, picking up Peter, and ran to the large stack of old hay bales.

'Over here,' came the cry (that only Peter could hear).

There, lying in a pile of hay was a fox cub. Mark froze.

'Mum told me not to get near foxes, they bite and have fleas,' he said screwing up his nose.

'Nonsense, he's only young and needs our help, he's injured,' Peter said.

The cub started talking to Peter, but Mark could not understand what the fox was saying.

'Peter, what's wrong?' Mark said.

'Oh sorry, I forgot you can't understand him. He's hurt his leg, so please put me down next to him.'

Mark hesitated and then put Peter on the ground, next to the cub.

'He's promised not to eat me, or bite you,' Peter said, 'he just wants to get back to his family. He said he was playing with his brothers late last night on the bales and was showing off. He climbed to the top one and slipped and fell. I think he has just twisted his leg,' said Peter. 'If he doesn't get home soon, his mum will miss him when she wakes up.'

'How come his brothers didn't help him?' Mark asked.

'They didn't know he had hurt himself. He's

the eldest and had told them to run back to the den and he would be back a bit later. He just wanted to look at the stars and the moon, as it was such a clear night,' Peter replied.

Mark nodded, understanding.

'Mark,' Peter said, 'this is where I need you to help me with my magic.'

Mark looked excitedly at Peter.

'Tell me what to do,' Mark said.

'Nothing too technical,' Peter said, 'just tap my back gently, three times.'

Mark did as he was told. Peter gave a little jerk. Mark thought he had seen Peter's back unzip but blinked and all was fine. Except now Peter had a red rucksack with a cross on it beside him. This bag was larger than him!

'Can you unzip my First Aid kit please?' Peter said, 'and pass me a bandage.'

It took Mark a few seconds to jump to attention and unzip the bag, as he was still trying to work out how it got there! The fox cub, now known as Finn, said he'd slipped a few hours ago.

'Oh,' said Peter, 'haven't you walked since then?' 'I took a few steps, but it was very painful,' said Finn.

Peter carefully and slowly moved Finn's front left leg.

'Wow,' said Finn, 'it feels like there is a healing warmth going through my leg.'

'That's because there is,' said Peter. 'The good news is,' said Peter, facing Mark, 'Finn hasn't broken it and the bruising is already coming out. It's just a bad sprain, so we will strap him up and help him home.'

Mark watched while Peter carefully bandaged Finn's leg. He stood silent, enchanted by the work of his little guinea pig, who was carefully running round Finn's leg with a crisp white bandage.

'There,' Peter said, 'all done. Finn, just check you feel comfy to move.'

Finn slowly got to his feet.

'That's amazing, I don't feel any pain.'

'That's good, a couple of days and you'll be as right as rain, but no mountaineering please,' Peter said.

'I won't' said Finn. 'I can't thank you enough, Peter.'

Peter nodded, 'Anytime.'

Mark had been so moved by what had just happened, he had completely forgotten the time. Looking at his watch he screeched, 'Peter! It's 1.40pm, I have to be home in five minutes, or mum will be furious.'

Peter gave Mark instructions to put him back in his pocket and then carry Finn back to

the entrance of his den, which would only take a couple of minutes.

'But Peter, where is your first aid kit?' Mark asked.

'All safe and sound,' Peter said, and with that they started to make their way to the den.

'Peter, can you tell Mark that it's just over there, by that large oak tree,' Finn said.

As Mark got nearer to the tree, he saw a well

hidden hole amongst the undergrowth. Mark carefully put Finn down.

'I'll be fine now. I can't thank you enough, come and visit me soon,' Finn said. 'Give me a couple of those *weet, weet, weets*, Peter, and I will come out and see you. I'll show mummy my bandage when she wakes up, she'll just be happy I'm safe.'

And with that, Finn carefully entered the den and disappeared out of sight. Mark lifted Peter out of his pocket.

'What a very kind and clever guinea pig you are,' he said smiling. 'I'm going to call you Peter Wee from now on, after all those strange weet noises you keep making.' He giggled out loud. 'Now we best run home, before I get into trouble. Hold on!' he said to Peter as he popped him back in his pocket.

'It is my birthday today after all!'

THE BIRTHDAY PARTY

Mark ran down the side of the house, through the back gate and into the garden. He needed to get Peter safely back in the hutch before his mother spotted him. Geraldine was already in the hutch and Benjamin was in the one next door. Geraldine seemed very pleased to see Peter, Mark thought, she sounded like she was purring.

'See you later, Peter Wee!' Mark shouted. 'I must dash.'

As Mark ran back to the house, he noticed the run had been moved. His brother's goal posts had been put on the lawn and various sized balloons and banners were hanging from the trees in the garden, all with the words HAPPY BIRTHDAY and SEVEN TODAY.

'Wow!' Mark thought. 'The best birthday ever and still more fun to come.'

His mother just pointed towards the stairs when she saw him.

'Your blue shirt is on your bed, and don't wear your best jeans, as you will wreck them if you start playing football with your friends.'

'Yes mum!' he shouted, as he legged it up the stairs.

Phew, he had gotten away with that, but probably only because it was his birthday. When he came back downstairs, Mark was quite pleased with himself, as he had even remembered to brush his hair.

His mum looked at him. 'How's your birthday so far then, son?'

'It's great mum, just great, I love being seven,' Mark replied.

On the kitchen table, there now lay a feast of various sandwiches, bowls of crisps, chicken drumsticks, pizza slices, carrots, hummus, sausage rolls and much more. His birthday cake took centre stage on the table. Mark thought it looked really scrummy. He ran down to the hutches with a couple of carrots and some of the guinea pig pellets in a bowl.

'Thanks,' said Peter Wee, 'we were getting a bit peckish, busy morning. Have a great party.'

'Will do,' Mark said as he skipped to the house.

A few minutes later Mark's friends, Josh, Carl and Sam, started to arrive, with presents under their arms. He was thrilled to find he had a book on guinea pig care from Josh, a huge bar of chocolate from Carl and a Lego super hero from Sam.

'Wow, thanks,' said Mark.

His brother Tom and sister Debbie came downstairs.

'Can we have a game of football before we eat, please mum?' said Mark.

'Go on then, but don't drink that cola while you are running around, it will only give you the hiccups.'

Mark giggled. They all ran outside, and Debbie and Mark were put in goal, while the other four just ran round passing the ball to each other. Quite a few goals were scored. Peter Wee kept shouting with enthusiasm at Mark.

'Dive Mark, save a few goals.' Mark giggled.

'Is there something wrong with your new guinea pig?' Carl asked. 'He hasn't stopped squeaking, is he in pain?'

'I don't think so' Mark replied, thinking quickly. 'I think he is just wanting me to save a few goals,' he said laughing. His friends laughed too.

'Five more minutes,' his mum called.

'Okay!' they all shouted.

With that, Carl got a bit more enthusiastic to score again before the game ended. He ran towards Mark, so quickly whilst dribbling the ball, that he slipped and fell and knocked his knee on the side of the garden path.
Everyone ran towards him, checking he was okay.

'It's fine, it's only a bump, it's my fault for wearing shorts.' Carl giggled.

'Mark, you can't be too sure. Run in and get a clean tea towel, pop some ice inside it, tie it up and pop it on Carl's knee!' Peter Wee shouted.

'Will do,' said Mark.

'Will do what?' said his friends all at once.

'Sorry,' said Mark, 'I was thinking out loud. I will just run inside and make you a cold pack for your knee, Carl. Won't be a minute,' he said

running off towards the house.

Mark came back with two antiseptic wipes from his mum, and a cold pack.

'Wow,' said his sister Debbie, 'where did you learn that?'

'Saw it on TV,' said Mark.

They all sat on the lawn, while Mark did his

first aid. Peter Wee was shouting instructions from the hutch.

'Wow,' said Tom, 'poor Gerald will have earache living with that. You best take Peter back to the shop and get a different one.'

Everyone laughed.

'I will go and check if he's okay,' Mark said, thinking, 'If only they knew my secret,' then adding, 'You all go in for our Birthday tea now, I'll be one minute, and don't forget to wash your hands to keep mum happy.' He went to visit Peter Wee.

'Well done, we'll make a doctor of you yet,' said Peter Wee.

'Peter Wee, they think you are ill squeaking like that,' Mark said laughing. 'You'll have to keep quiet for a bit now. I'm off for my birthday tea, I will see you later.'

The birthday food was amazing, and everyone ate far too much. 'Happy Birthday' was sung during the candle blowing and they all managed to fit in a piece of birthday cake, although they all said they were now at bursting point. Afterwards, it was decided that Mark, Carl, Josh and Sam would go to Mark's room and play on the XBox until their parents arrived to collect them. Debbie and Tom went to their rooms, leaving Mum and Dad to clear up. At 7pm Mark's friends were collected.

'Thanks, mum and dad, I have had the best birthday ever,' Mark said as he stood in the lounge.

'You're welcome,' they replied.

'I will just go and check on Peter Wee,' he said, yawning.

'Peter Wee?' his mum said laughing.

'Yes, he goes *weet, weet, weet,* all the time,' said Mark.

His parents laughed.

Mark ran down to the hutches. Peter Wee and Geraldine were in the upstairs compartment, snuggled up together in the new hammock that Mark's mum had made for them. It hung from two large brass hooks that his dad had screwed in.

'Hi,' said Peter Wee, yawning. 'What a great day.'

'Yes,' said Mark 'the best birthday ever. Sleep well.'

He pulled the curtain over both hutches and returned to the house.

'I think it's bedtime,' he said, as he plodded up the stairs, smiling.

THE DOG NEXT DOOR

Mark and Peter Wee spent the next few days of
the Easter holidays going for their usual walks
over to the field and playing on the bales. They
would often pop over to visit Finn at his den.
Peter Wee would make his *weet, weet* noise and
Finn would come out to see them. He was fully
recovered from his fall now and loved their visits.
Occasionally, Finn's mum gave him permission

to play with them in the bales, but on strict instructions, if they saw farmer James, that he had to come straight home. On the first day, Finn's mum came out to thank Peter Wee. Mark was a little scared, as she was much bigger than Finn. But now he was growing up he tried not to look too nervous and just smiled, while she chatted with Peter Wee. Afterwards, Peter Wee always explained to Mark what they were talking about.

For a couple of days over Easter, as the weather was so lovely, Mark went out for a ride with his family to the seaside at Whitstable. Peter Wee was always very upset as he couldn't go with him, and when Mark returned, Peter Wee was always very quiet and sulking. As soon as Mark was home from the family outing, he put Peter Wee and Geraldine into the run and created their own little seaside retreat. He made them an umbrella out of some of their hay and a stick from the garden, their own beach from some sand found in the corner of the garden, and a shallow paddling pool made from one of his dad's greenhouse trays. He would then cut them some cucumber into the shape of ice cream cones. He had even found them two little dolls' sun hats in his sister Debbie's old toy box she no longer played with. Peter Wee and Geraldine would squeal and *weet* with joy, as they dabbled their feet in the tray of water. Mark sat on the side of the run and laughed until his sides hurt watching them play.

'I'm just popping into the house for some water,' Mark said, 'it's so hot today.'

'Right you are,' said Peter Wee, splashing about in the tray.

As Mark returned to the run with a large glass of iced water, his brother Tom appeared. He looked at the guinea pigs in their hats and the little beach scene and turned to Mark.

'You really have lost the plot, don't forget it is

your turn to clean them out, I'm going to play on my computer.'

And with that Tom walked towards the house. Mark thought it was always his turn nowadays to clean the hutches, but he didn't mind.

Mark's mum had said it was twenty-two degrees today, which is very warm for April, so he put the old curtain over the corner of the run to give them some shade.

'Thanks, we were getting a bit warm with all this fur,' said Peter Wee.

Just then, there was a very loud barking noise, which was coming over the hedge from next door.

'That must be Pickle,' Mark said to Peter Wee. 'He's Mr Brown's dog – he's a Bassett Hound. In fact, he looks a lot like you, Peter Wee, very short legs and a long chubby brown and white body,' he said laughing.

With that there was a crunching sound at the base of the hedge and Pickle had squeezed himself underneath into Mark's garden. Peter Wee and Geraldine stood very still, in case he headed towards them. But he had his eye on something else! Pickle was chasing a cat that had quickly jumped up into one of his Dad's apple trees. He was now running round and round the base of the tree, barking his head off and jumping up towards the cat, although his body was only a couple of inches off the ground. Mark ran towards

Pickle, trying to catch him, but they just ended up playing chase instead, round and round the tree. When Mark thought he could just catch Pickle, he darted in the opposite direction.

Mark stood still watching Pickle. Suddenly the dog came to an abrupt stop, his legs seemed to buckle underneath him and he was breathing really heavily. Mark stood there a bit shocked.

'Oh no, have I killed him?' he said out loud.

Peter Wee was squealing at Mark. 'Quick Mark, lift me out of the run, I need to get my First Aid Kit.'

Mark jumped into action and grabbed Peter Wee from the run. He carefully placed him on the ground next to Pickle, whose tongue now looked really long as he was breathing so badly. Mark carefully patted Peter Wee on the back three times, as Peter Wee gave instructions. Mark looked more closely this time and it honestly did, Mark thought, look like Peter Wee's back unzipped very quickly. Again, there appeared the red rucksack with the cross. But it's bigger than Peter Wee, Mark thought. 'Pass me the thermometer please, you will have to help me lift his jaw open, I'm not strong enough,' said Peter Wee.

Mark grabbed the thermometer and Peter Wee carefully placed it near Pickle's mouth. Mark was very impressed as it gave out a red light.

'Digital and infrared,' said Peter Wee, looking proud.

Peter Wee then carefully climbed onto

Pickle's shoulders and placed the thermometer in Pickle's ear.

'His temperature is a tiny bit high, it should be about 39.2 degrees celsius and it is 39.5' he said to Mark. 'Would you please run and get a bucket of lukewarm water and a couple of old towels.'

Mark ran to the house. Peter Wee started rubbing Pickle's nose.

'You'll be fine, Pickle, you've just overdone it a bit and got a little too warm.'

'Thank you,' said Pickle. 'Wow! Your paws feel as though they are cooling me down!'

'That's because they are,' said Peter Wee, 'now keep breathing as deeply as you can Pickle. In and out, in and out. Well done,' said Peter Wee.

With that, Mark was back with the towels.

'Mark, soak the towels in the bucket please and then carefully lay them over Pickle,' Peter Wee instructed.

Mark carried out his duties and then stroked Pickle's head.

'Oh, Peter Wee, you are so clever,' Mark said, 'He is looking better already.'

Pickle confirmed he was feeling much better, with Peter Wee letting Mark know what was said.

'Peter Wee,' said Mark, 'mum saw Pickle lying in the garden and has gone to find Mr Brown, I need to quickly pop you back in the run.'

'Right you are,' said Peter Wee.

Mark lifted Peter Wee up, giving him a big kiss and stroking him as he popped him back in the run.

The First Aid Kit was nowhere to be seen, but Mark knew better than to ask where it had gone. He just smiled and ran back to sit with Pickle, just as his mum and Mr Brown came up the garden path. Pickle was now back on his feet, licking Mark all over.

'He's okay Mr Brown, he just got a bit warm chasing a cat,' Mark said.

'Oh, thank you so much Mark, how did you know how to cool him down?'

'Seen it on the TV,' Mark said smiling and looking over to Peter Wee, who winked back at him.

Mr Brown picked up Pickle and thanked Mark again. He said he would mend the hole in the hedge and pop Pickle in his basket in their kitchen, where it was nice and cool and he could rest. Mum patted Mark on the shoulder.

'Well done Mark for your quick thinking,' she said with a smile.

Later that evening, Mr Brown popped round to say Pickle was fine and had eaten his tea. He then handed Mark a huge box, inside of which was the most amazing chocolate pizza.

'Wow, thank you so much,' said Mark.
'NO THANK YOU' replied Mr Brown.

THE ROBIN AND THE RHUBARB

For Mark the Easter Holiday had been amazing, but tomorrow it was time to go back to school. It was early evening and he had strict instructions to have a bath, lay out his uniform for the morning and pack his school bag.

'But mum, I must just go and tuck Peter Wee in first, he's really going to miss me while I am at school,' said Mark.

'Mark, he is only a guinea pig,' his mother replied, 'besides, you will have to feed and clean him out after school and can play with him then, as long as you have done your homework first.'

'Great,' said Mark, thinking, 'he's not just any old guinea pig, he's magical and he's mine.'

Mark walked down the garden to the hutches. Peter Wee was curled up next to Geraldine. 'I am really going to miss you while you are at school, Mark,' said Peter Wee in a sad voice. 'I am so glad I have Geraldine for company.'

'I will be home before you know it, mum has promised to lift you both into the run each day as long as it doesn't rain. Please don't wriggle too much, as she is a bit scared of you,' said Mark, giggling.

'We promise,' said Peter Wee.

'Good night,' said Mark, giving them both a stroke before putting the latch down securely and pulling the old curtain over them.

'Good night,' replied Peter Wee in a very sad voice.

Mark thought he heard Peter Wee blow his nose as he walked away, but shook his head thinking he must be imagining it. He went up to his bedroom, wishing he could have his Easter Holiday all over again. He got into bed and soon fell into a deep sleep, dreaming of all the fun times he had enjoyed with his magical guinea pig.

The next morning, Mrs James and Josh arrived on the doorstep at 7.30am sharp, as they always did on a school day. Mrs James walked them to the village school every day, before she went home and worked on the farm. Mark's mum was in charge of picking them up. She would normally walk, but occasionally she would drive up to collect them both after school. Mark liked it when his mum drove. They were always tired in the afternoon, especially if they had been doing a sports lesson.

It was nearly a mile to walk to school. This morning, Mark and Josh never even noticed the walk as they were chatting so much, while Mrs James went off in front. Mark had to be so careful not to mention Peter Wee too often, in case Josh suspected something. So, he chatted about his trips to Whitstable and asked Josh what he had been doing.

Josh seemed somewhat upset that Mark hadn't been round to play on the farm, like he usually did in the school holidays. Mark apologised and said he would come over soon. He said cleaning out two hutches and looking after three pets (as his sister and brother did not bother much anymore), had taken up quite a lot of his time.

Carl and Sam were already in the playground. They both grinned from ear to ear when they saw Mark and Josh coming through the gate. The four boys had five minutes to play tag before the school bell. They waved goodbye to Mrs James and then started chasing each other.

Luckily the school day passed quickly and soon the bell was ringing for the end of the last lesson – Maths (not Mark's favourite). His brother Tom was good at maths and often explained it to Mark while he helped him with his homework. But that was only on the occasions that Tom could be bothered. Mark's mum was at the front gate and yippee she had the car, even though it was a lovely sunny day.

'Thanks mum,' said Mark as he jumped in the back. Josh leapt into the front.

'You're lucky,' said Mark's mum 'I have just been to the supermarket to stock up. You can help me put it away when we get home.'

'But mum! Peter Wee has been on his own all day.'

Josh gave out a little laugh.

'I think that guinea pig has you wrapped around his little finger!' said Mark's mum.

They dropped Josh off at the farm gates, Mark waving enthusiastically.

'See you in the morning, Josh,' Mark said. In a couple of minutes they pulled into the drive.

'Peter Wee and Gerald are in the run with Benjamin,' said Mark's mum, 'so you can at least help me carry the shopping in and take your uniform off before you see them.'

Mark opened the boot and lifted out two large shopping bags, which were nearly as heavy as he was, although he was determined to carry both at once to save time. He put them onto the kitchen floor and then ran up the stairs to get changed. He quickly put his school trousers over the back of the chair, threw his school shirt towards his laundry bin (missing badly), laughed and left it on the floor while he pulled on his tee shirt and shorts. He ran into the kitchen and grabbed a glass of squash. His mum just tutted as he ran outside.

Calling after him, she said, 'Do you have any homework?'

But Mark was already out of sight. Benjamin stamped his foot on the grass, as Mark had made him jump, while Geraldine and Peter Wee gave out loads of *weet, weet, weets* of pure joy when they saw Mark approaching.

'Welcome home, Mark,' said Peter Wee, 'we've missed you.'

Mark opened the lid on the run and picked up Peter Wee, stroking him fondly.

'I missed you too,' said Mark.

Peter Wee started purring and weeting so
loud that Benjamin stamped his foot again.

'What's wrong with him?' asked Mark.

'He's a bit jealous. Debbie hardly strokes and
plays with him anymore,' said Peter Wee.

'Wow, you're getting very heavy Peter Wee,
you and Geraldine are putting on weight, I will
have to put you both on diets,' Mark said laughing.

'I don't know why,' said Peter Wee, 'as we eat mainly fruit and vegetables and they are good for us.'

Mark lifted Peter Wee back into the run and watched them, laughing, while they chased each other round and round (or did their circuits!). Benjamin just sat in the middle of them rubbing his ears.

'Five more minutes while I clean out your hutches, then it will be time for my tea. I'm starving,' Mark said.

'Okey dokey. What have we got for our tea?' asked Peter Wee.

'Your favourite pellets and a lovely fresh carrot,' said Mark.

'Yum,' said Peter Wee, squeaking with delight.

Mark had finished cleaning the hutches, lifting Benjamin first. There was a lovely fresh carrot and hay as well. Next it was Geraldine's turn. Wow, she weighs a ton Mark thought, but didn't dare say it out loud. Then he lifted Peter Wee.

'Chubby little friend,' he said laughing, tickling Peter Wee's tummy. 'I'll pop back to tuck you in later' Mark said before running back to the house.

The next few days followed a very similar routine, every afternoon after school Mark would visit Peter Wee as soon as he could. Some days, if he had homework, he had to sit at the kitchen table, with his mother watching over him until he finished. She always checked that he had completed everything before he was allowed in the garden.

One afternoon, Mark and Josh had been picked up by car again as there had been quite a bad thunderstorm at lunchtime. When Mark got home, he found Peter Wee and Geraldine snuggled up in the hammock, shaking. The wind and rain had been so strong that it had made the main part of the hutch wet.

'It's okay, I'm home now. The storm has finished,' he said to them.

'Thank goodness, that was quite scary,' said Peter Wee.

Mark left them curled up in the hammock, while he removed the damp straw and replaced it with fresh dry straw. Suddenly, Mark had an idea. His mum had popped round to Mr Brown's with a homemade cake and so he said to Peter Wee, 'We are going on an adventure!' Mark untucked the bottom of his tee shirt and placed Geraldine and Peter Wee inside making them a hammock.

'Keep still, so I don't drop you both.'

Peter Wee squealed with delight, *weet, weet*.

Mark carefully carried both of them up to his bedroom and placed them on the bed, where they both started running from one end to the other, bouncing on the mattress.

'Whatever you do, don't make a mess, as mum would kill me,' Mark said.

'Wow,' said Peter Wee, 'can I look out of the glass, Mark? Can you see our hutches from here?'

Mark carefully lifted Peter Wee onto the windowsill. Peter Wee ran along the sill knocking all Mark's lego toys to the floor.

'Oi! It took me ages to build those. Don't you fall!' he said laughing.

Peter Wee was staring out towards a large tree trunk in the corner of the garden, that stood about six feet high.

'That was struck by lightning years ago, before we lived here,' Mark told Peter Wee, as they both looked over at the tree.

All of a sudden, Peter Wee started *weet, weeting* at the top of his voice.

'There is something wrong. Rosie the robin has a nest in that tree, I can hear her crying. Mark, you have to get me there now. Geraldine, stay on the bed and don't move,' Peter Wee instructed.

With that Mark picked up Peter Wee, grabbing his anorak from the hook as they went through the kitchen and headed to the tree. It was far too high for Mark to see anything, but Peter Wee was *weet, weeting* at the top of his voice. Mark thought he could hear a bird calling, singing, or shouting? He wasn't sure.

'Mark, Rosie's nest was knocked sideways by the strong winds earlier, she was trying to level it back up, but she wasn't strong enough.'

'It tipped even more and two of her eggs have

just rolled out of the nest. She says three eggs are still safe. She's so upset, we have to help her,' said Peter Wee. 'Mark, can you lift me as high as you can, to that big branch and I will climb up and help Rosie to see if I can help level the nest with my weight.'

'You'll easily do that with your tummy,' Mark said laughing.

'This is no time for jokes,' replied Peter Wee sternly.

'Sorry,' said Mark. 'But guinea pigs can't climb!'

'Magical ones can,' said Peter. 'Now Mark, you are in charge of finding the eggs. Tread very carefully and when you find them don't touch them,' instructed Peter Wee.

Mark started to look on the ground. At the base of the tree there was a huge clump of rhubarb his father had planted a few years ago. The leaves were large and crumpled and inside the largest leaf lay a small white matt egg. It was just balanced in the joint of the leaf at the top of the stem. As Mark moved round very slowly, looking at the rest of the leaves, he found the second egg, again resting in the cup of the rhubarb leaf.

'I've found them! They don't look broken as luckily they are resting on top of these large rhubarb leaves!' shouted Mark proudly.

'Well done, we just have to find a way of getting them back to Rosie's nest,' replied Peter Wee.

As Mark looked up at the broken tree stump, he saw Peter Wee sliding down the bark of the tree, like it was a fireman's pole. As soon as Mark could reach him, he lifted Peter Wee into the safety of his hands.

'Wow, Peter Wee, you are so clever,' Mark said.

'No time for chat now, Mark,' said Peter Wee, 'can you put me on the ground please? I need my first aid kit.'

Mark now knew what to do. He carefully put Peter Wee on the ground and tapped his back gently three times. It always amazed him what happened next, but Peter Wee was shouting out instructions to him, so he had no time to marvel at the magic.

Mark ran to the hutch and carefully unhooked the hammock his mother had made. He grabbed a small handful of hay and ran back to Peter Wee.

'Thanks,' said Peter Wee, who was now rummaging about in the red first aid kit beside him. He pulled out a bandage, some cotton wool and some sticky tape.

'Mark, this is really important, you must do exactly as I say,' said Peter Wee.

Mark nodded, looking quite worried. Rosie was peering over the top of the tree stump, in complete silence. Peter Wee started the complicated instructions.

'Lift me back up to the branch please, so I can help Rosie pull the hammock up. Take some cotton wool and carefully make it into a square, big enough to wrap up each egg. Don't touch the eggs with your hands, just with the cotton wool, as Rosie might reject them if they smell of you,' said Peter Wee.

Mark screwed up his face, with a worried look.

'The eggs are very fragile, so don't squeeze them. Lay them, one at a time, in the hammock.'

Mark concentrated and slowly did as Peter Wee said.

'Build the hay up around them, so they don't crack or knock each other on the way up. There is a bandage beside you – tie it as tight as you can, using one end, so it makes the hammock into a bag around the eggs, leaving them room to breathe.'

Mark took a deep breath, whilst carefully holding the hammock in place.

'Use the sticky tape to secure the bandage in place, I can gnaw it all off when it's safely in the nest. Well done,' said Peter Wee, looking down at Mark who was carefully following the instructions.

'I'm trying not to shake. I'm only seven!' Mark cried out.

'Now, hold the bag still in one hand and pass me the other end of the bandage,' said Peter Wee.

Mark, carefully and slowly, did as he was instructed. As Peter Wee got hold of the bandage in his teeth, it seemed to mysteriously wrap itself around Peter Wee's body until it was securely tied in place.

'Wow,' said Mark, 'that really is magic.'

Peter Wee then very slowly started to climb the tree stump, tightly gripping the bark with his claws, the hammock slowly sliding up behind him. Mark thought Peter Wee looked more like a monkey than a small guinea pig. He felt helpless below, so he put his hands out, just in case his amazing friend slipped.

As Peter neared the nest, Rosie too started pulling the bandage and hammock to safety with her tiny beak. It seemed to take forever, but finally the hammock had reached the top and Rosie and Peter Wee started to undo the tape and bandage.

Mark jumped up and down, shouting, 'Way to go!'

'Rosie, you sit next to the other three eggs, so I don't knock them,' said Peter Wee.

And with that, all five eggs were safely back where they belonged Rosie then started to half fly, half dance. Mark thought it sounded like Rosie was laughing or chuckling. She wrapped her wings round Peter Wee and gave him a huge peck on the cheek. Fortunately, Mark couldn't see this from down below, much to Peter Wee's relief, as he was quite embarrassed.

'Take care Rosie, let me know when they hatch,' said Peter Wee.

'God bless you. You are amazing Peter Wee,' said Rosie.

And with that, Peter Wee was sliding down the tree again into the safety of Mark's hands.

'Peter Wee, you are one in a million,' said Mark.

'I think you will find I am one in ten million!'
Peter replied, correcting him, and they both
laughed.

They were both soon brought straight back
down to earth, when from the house Mark's mum
started screaming at the top of her voice.

'Mark, get in here now!'

'Ouch, I'm in trouble now,' he said.

In their haste to help Rosie, they had forgotten that Geraldine was still on Mark's bed.

'Crikey, I think mum has just found her,' said Mark.

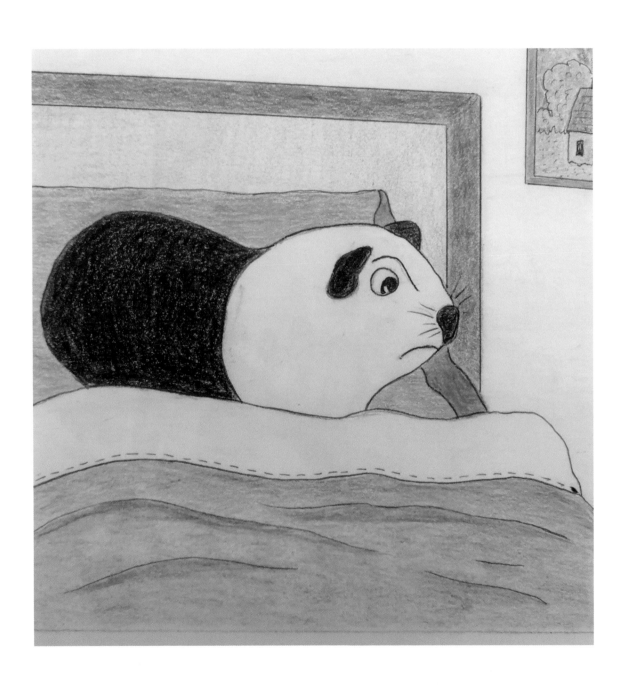

TOM'S BIG SURPRISE

It was half term and May Spring Bank Holiday. Mark and Peter Wee had enjoyed the last few days spending time over at the field with Finn. He had grown very big now, making Mark a little more nervous of him. Finn had to be very careful when playing in daylight with them, as although the old hay bales were still stacked high and provided shelter, the field had just been harvested and Mr James was often seen driving past in his tractor. Mark always waved at him enthusiastically.

On one occasion, Josh was on the tractor and jumped off to see Mark. He had to quickly shove Peter Wee into his lunch bag, squashing Peter Wee's face as he half zipped it up. After five minutes Mark had to make an excuse that he was needed back at the house to play football with his brother, Tom. After waving goodbye to Josh and running as fast as he could out of Josh's sight, Mark was relieved to find Peter Wee was fine, even if he was slightly sticky from the melon slice that had been in the bottom of the lunch bag. Peter Wee took great delight in licking all four paws as Mark lifted him out. He had not only eaten all the melon flesh, there were even tiny teeth marks in the rind.

Mark and Peter Wee had also been following the progress of the hatching of Rosie's chicks over the last few days. They were thrilled when all five had emerged from their shells safely, only a few days after the dramatic rescue of the eggs. Peter Wee had asked Rosie if it was okay if Mark took a few photos once the chicks started learning to fly for his school project, which she agreed to, so Mark and Peter Wee would sit near the old tree stump, while Rosie showed her chicks how to fly. Mark, always with a camera in hand, loved taking photos. Quite often they were a little bit blurred as he and Peter Wee would get into a fit of giggles as the smallest baby robin, called Reg, would look like a really wobbly trapeze artist and then wouldn't let go of the branch. Finally, Rosie would end up pushing him off the branch, so he had no choice but to try and fly.

Reg always landed a bit clumsily on top of the hutches, which was great for Mark's photography and close up shots. He was often still laughing at Reg's flying attempts, so not that many of the photos were clear enough for his project. Reg was getting quite tame and liked Mark to put a little bird seed on the hutch after his high-flying act.

Rosie and Peter Wee often chatted and Mark had to remind Peter Wee to tell him what had been said, as he didn't understand. He was very sad to learn, when Peter Wee explained it to him, that there were only a few days left before the baby robins would fly off to make their own lives away from the garden.

'This is because they are territorial,' Peter Wee explained. 'This means that they would fight if they stayed living in the same garden.' Mark nodded, pretending to understand, but was a little confused by this. When Mark showed his mum his photos, she told him there was an old story that robins were meant to bring you luck and if someone you knew had gone to heaven, people believed that they might come back as a robin to look over you. Mark's mum said that it might be her sister, Olive, who had sadly died of cancer last year. Mark was thrilled to think Rosie was his Auntie Olive, as he had loved her very much and she always had a way of making him laugh.

The bit about robins bringing you luck did come true for Mark a few weeks later. His 'Robin's Nest' school project received the highest score in class. He had been presented with a trophy and a big box of chocolates in front of the whole school assembly, much to his brother Tom's disgust.

Mark had spent yesterday over with Josh on the farm. He had even had a ride on Josh's pony, Magic. He felt very high up and only let Josh lead Magic into a walk and then a trot, as he felt very wobbly and kept slipping out of the saddle and was glad when it was time to get off, but thanked Josh politely for the experience. He was quite surprised when he had told Peter Wee he was going to the farm for a few hours. Peter Wee had not gone into his normal sulk and had said he was quite happy to be with Geraldine.

As it was the May Spring Bank holiday, his parents had organised a barbecue with some of their neighbours and Mark's aunts and uncles. They were all due to start arriving in half an hour, so Peter Wee, Geraldine and Benjamin had to be put in the hutches, fed and the run moved out of the way.

Mark's dad had already lit the barbecue and the flames were heading high into the sky. Peter Wee started *weet, weeting* at the top of his voice, shouting.

'Fire! Fire!' although only Mark could understand him.

Mark had to quickly run over to him and explain that it was fine and only a barbecue.

When Mark got back to the barbecue, his dad said, 'That is the noisiest guinea pig I have ever laid eyes on. What's wrong with him now?'

'I think he's grumpy, because I put him in the hutch earlier than normal. He has a mind of his own,' Mark said laughing.

'You're not kidding,' his dad said, laughing too.

His brother Tom and sister Debbie appeared, carrying plates and cutlery and put them on the long trestle table that had been placed on the lawn. It was already laden with glasses, bowls of

crisps and peanuts, ketchup, brown sauce, a huge plate of various salads and a stack of burger and hot dog rolls. Mark's stomach started to rumble. The barbecue was now flameless and ready to cook the chicken, sausages and burgers, according to Mark's dad.

'Great, I'm starving,' said Mark.

'You have always had hollow legs,' his dad replied.

His Auntie Paula and Uncle Andrew had just arrived with flowers and a big bottle of prosecco. Next came his Uncle Mike, who was often quite sad nowadays since losing his wife, Mark's Auntie Olive. He lifted Mark up and threw him over his shoulder.

'How's my favourite little nephew?' he said to Mark.

'Getting taller, Uncle Mike,' Mark replied, giggling.

Then Mr Brown arrived from next door, with Pickle his dog. 'Wow, that might be a bad idea. Pickle had a reputation of being a naughty dog and there was lots of food lying around,' Mark thought. He grinned to himself. Tom caught his eye and grinned back, thinking the same thing. Mr and Mrs James were next to arrive with Josh.

'Hi,' Mark said to Josh, 'hope you're hungry.'

The sizzling food was starting to smell delicious, his dad was very busy turning the burgers and sausages and trying to drink a large bottle of beer at the same time. Everyone was drinking and talking. Mark jokingly asked his mum for a beer, but she passed him a glass of diet cola and gave him a scolding look. The barbecue was in full swing, his dad's favourite nineties music on the CD player. Mark and Josh were running up and down the garden path, while Pickle was barking his head off. Then all of a sudden Rosie swooped down, brushing the top of Mark's hair.

'Wow,' said Josh, laughing, 'a dive-bombing robin.'

Rosie was squeaking and shouting at the top of her voice. Peter Wee was also *weet, weeting* – 'Help! Help!' at the top of his guinea pig voice.

Fortunately, just as the CD that had been playing ended, Pickle stopped barking long enough for Mark to hear Peter Wee's cry for help and he knew something was wrong. Mark ran to the hutches, with Josh close behind on his heels.

'What's wrong?' said Josh, 'Your guinea pig is making such a racket.' 'I'm not sure,' said Mark, puffing as he arrived at the hutch.

'Oh Mark, thank goodness, I have been calling you for ages. I was going to tell you next week, but it's all happening sooner than I thought,' explained Peter Wee in a high-pitched squeak.

'What's happening?' said Mark, alarmed that Peter Wee had kept something from him. He thought they were best friends and did not have secrets.

'It's Geraldine, she's pregnant and having our babies NOW!' said Peter Wee, in a hysterical voice.

Mark stood silent for a couple of minutes, trying to take in what he had just been told. He opened the door and there was Geraldine, laying on her side puffing and grunting.

'Oh,' said Josh, 'is Gerald dying?'

'I don't think so!' said Mark thinking quickly,

'I have been reading that guinea pig care book you gave me for my birthday, and I think Gerald is a Geraldine and having babies.'

'Wow,' said Josh, 'amazing, can I watch?'

'Mark, send Josh to get Tom,' Peter Wee *weet, weeted*, to Mark 'I need to talk to you alone.'

Mark asked Josh if he would get Tom and give him the surprising news. Luckily, Tom was nowhere to be seen, which might give them a bit of extra time, especially if he was in his bedroom.

'Mark,' said Peter Wee, 'Listen carefully. I can't get my first aid kit out, there are too many humans around. Can you lift some of the hay from the front of the hutch and carefully build it round Geraldine please, so the babies have a soft landing.'

'How many are there?' said Mark.

'We won't know until they are born,' said Peter Wee. 'Also, have you got a clean tissue in your pocket?' Peter Wee asked.

'Yes,' said Mark.

'Can you please wet it, using our water bottle. I will place it on Geraldine's head to cool her down a bit,' said Peter Wee.

Mark did as instructed, and Peter Wee carefully laid the damp tissue between her ears.

'There's nothing else we can do now, except give her some privacy, it won't be long now,' Peter Wee confirmed.

Mark looked concerned.

'Animals aren't like humans when they have

babies, we don't make too much fuss. We are used to being on our own, no doctors and nurses, Geraldine is fine. We just wait for the squeaking of the babies,' said Peter Wee.

With that, Peter Wee seemed to realise what was about to happen.

'I am going to be a DAD!' he said.

Mark watched Peter Wee closely. He first did what can only be described as a somersault and then lay upside down in the remaining bedding wiggling his legs in the air.

'Are you OK, Peter Wee?' Mark asked in a concerned voice.

'Yes,' said Peter Wee, 'just SOOOO excited.'

Josh was running back down the garden, with Tom at his side.

'What is all this about Gerald having babies? He's just been eating too much. You're always feeding them, Mark,' said Tom in a grumpy voice.

'Tom, you'll believe me any minute now,' said Mark, confidently.

And, just as he said it, there was a small squeaking noise from the enclosed side of the hutch, then some much louder squeaking and grunting (that Mark guessed was Geraldine), followed by more mouse-like tiny squeaks. Peter Wee seemed to catapult back into the main hutch.

'THREE! I HAVE THREE CHILDREN!' he shouted.

Mark gasped out loud.

'I think the babies have been born by all the noises we've been hearing,' he said quickly, still in shock.

'The shop assistant promised me my guinea pig was definitely a boy,' Tom replied, still not believing his younger brother.

Next, Mark carefully and quietly lifted the latch on the hutch bedroom compartment and opened the door slightly. Amidst all the hay lay Geraldine and three wet, sticky balls of different coloured moving fluff. Josh stood behind Mark with his mouth wide open. Tom pushed Mark out of the way.

'Let me see,' he said in his older brother's tone.

As Mark stood back a little, Tom stood staring down at the three amazing miracles of fluff.

'WOWZER,' he said and then stood perfectly still, staring down at the three new babies.

Mark picked up Peter Wee and said, 'What an amazing little guinea pig you have turned out to be. We are going to have some wonderful adventures with your new family.'

'I love you with all my heart Peter Wee, you're the best'

With that, he turned to Tom and Josh and said in a very grown-up manner, for someone who was only seven, 'I think we should let them all rest for a while now and come back later. Peter Wee will let me know if he needs us. Race you both back to tell the others the news, and by the way, the biggest beef burger is mine!' Mark said laughing.

THE END

To be continued...